With special thanks to The Tiburon Peninsula Foundation, without whom this book would not have been possible.
The Board: Mogens Bach, Piper Berger, Robin Daly, Leslie Doyle, David Holscher, Art Kern, Ed Lynch, Jim Mitchell,
Arlene Nielsen, Arno Rayner, Steve Sears, Peyton Stein and especially—Larry Smith, who has been our champion
throughout; and to George Gnoss whose legal counsel has been invaluable.

— Christopher Cerf and Paige Peterson

The Tiburon Peninsula Foundation wishes to thank the following generous benefactors:

Jennifer Peak Barker
The Belvedere Land Company
Chong Cook and Sam
Robin Snow Daly
Fred Gellert Family Foundation
Sallie and Dick Griffith
Katharine Hotchkis Johnson
Arthur Kern in memory of Mara Kern
William and Gretchen Kimball Fund
The Nielsen Family—Chip, Arlene, Karla, Megan and Jeff
The Dennis and Carol Ann Rockey Fund
Gary and Cathy Spratling

For The Tiburon Peninsula Foundation

A Cerf & Peterson Book

Produced and distributed in 2014 by
Welcome Books®
An imprint of Welcome Enterprises, Inc.
6 West 18th Street
New York, NY 10011
(212) 989-3200; Fax (212) 989-3205
www.welcomebooks.com

Editor: Katrina Fried
Designer: Kate DeWitt
Editorial Assistant: Maren Gregerson

Design copyright © 2014 by Welcome Enterprises, Inc.
Text and illustration copyright © 2014 by The Tiburon
Peninsula Foundation

Library of Congress Cataloging-in-Publication data on file

ISBN: 978-1-59962-130-2

First Edition
10 9 8 7 6 5 4 3 2 1

Printed in Singapore

DEDICATION

This is the true story of a sway-backed horse named Blackie who stood in his pasture beside San Francisco Bay for the last 28 years of his 40-year life.

For

Alexandra, William, Peter Cary and Drew

Brianna, Devon, Kylee and Wyatt

And for Robin Daly, with love and profound gratitude for all you've done for Blackie

BLACK
THE HORSE WHO STOOD STILL

written by CHRISTOPHER CERF *and* PAIGE PETERSON

illustrated by PAIGE PETERSON

welcome
BOOKS

NEW YORK

In a pasture in Kansas
    one early spring morn,
A horse quite unlike
    other horses was born.
His coat was coal black
    so they named the horse "Blackie,"
And before very long folks found out
    he was wacky!

See, most colts are frisky

but Blackie was not.

Blackie liked **standing still!**

Yes, he liked it a lot!

"What's the hurry?" thought Blackie.

"There's so much to see,

Standing here in the **shade** of a juniper tree….

There are hawks, there are rabbits,
there's freshly-mown hay,
And **sunsets to watch**
at the end of the day.
So I don't want to gallop, I don't want to
race. Let the other colts move—
I'll just **stand in one place!**"

Now most of the people where Blackie
        was bred,
Felt that Blackie was useless—and here's
        what they said:
"What good is a horse that won't run and
        won't jump—
A horse who just stands in one place
        like a lump?"

But one day a rodeo cowboy came by,
And said, "Blackie, I'm willing to
give you a try…
Roping bulls at a gallop is tricky indeed…
But a horse who stands still?
Hey, you're just what I need!"

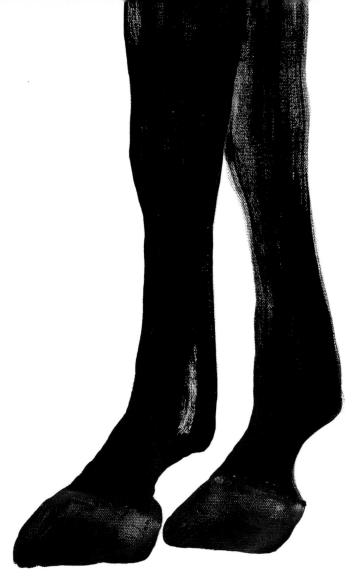

"I won't leave this field!" Blackie thought.
"I hate change!
I won't budge from my sweet Kansas
home on the range!
Moving's out of the question from my point of view,
'Cause I might miss the world passing by if I do."

"If I gave you a big cube
          of sugar to lick,
Would that change your mind?
          Would that do the trick?"
Asked the cowboy, but Blackie just
          shook his head, "No!
I'm a horse who stays put, and I'm
          not going to go!"

But the man said, "Well, let's see
          what else I can find…
Hmm, these carrots and apples
          might just change your mind!"
"Sugar, carrots, AND apples!"
          thought Blackie, "How tasty!
I think my refusal to go was too hasty!"

KANSAS

And he grabbed all the food, and he wolfed it all down,
And he got in the truck, and they drove out of town!
For hundreds of miles, they sped on **without rest**...

...Till they reached California—a state way out west!

The rodeo man had a house in Salinas.
When they got there he said,
    "Blackie, hey, just between us,
The rodeo here is the best that I know
So let's go right over and put on a show!"

They **arrived** at the rodeo just after two,
And the rider told Blackie just what they would do:
"I'll sit on your back; you'll stand still as a **statue**,
And I'll rope all the bulls as they come running at you!"
And stand still he did, and it made him **a hero** —
His rider roped **ten bulls** — the others roped zero!

The crowd was **astounded**. They cheered with great force,
For the new roping **champ** and his standing-still horse!

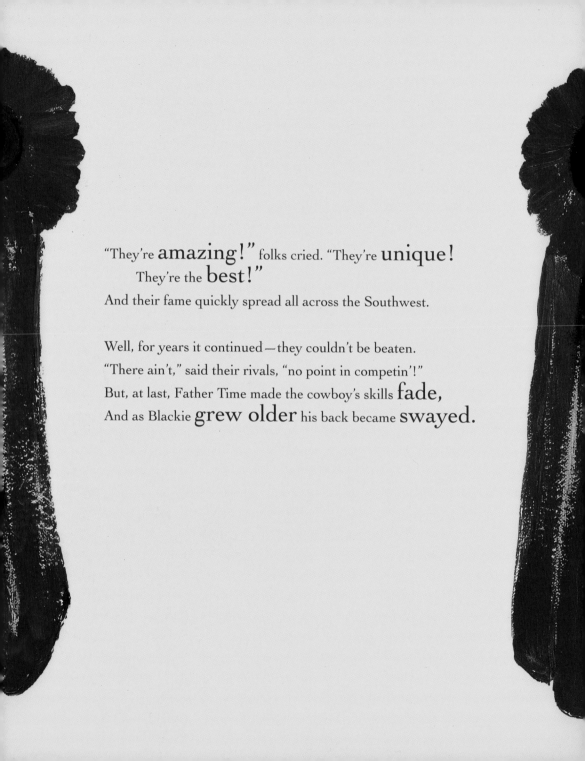

"They're amazing!" folks cried. "They're unique!
They're the best!"
And their fame quickly spread all across the Southwest.

Well, for years it continued—they couldn't be beaten.
"There ain't," said their rivals, "no point in competin'!"
But, at last, Father Time made the cowboy's skills fade,
And as Blackie grew older his back became swayed.

So the cowboy **retired,** and he fought back a tear,
And said "Blackie, this **ends** your bull-roping career,
'Cause not one other rider has got enough skill,
To rope bulls from a sway-back old horse who stands still.
There's **no work** for you here, but I've found a great **remedy:**
An exciting **new job** on patrol at **Yosemite**! "

Blackie neighed in a tone that was most **disapproving.**
"Patrolling," he thought, "Can't be done without moving!
So **I won't leave** this spot! You can try what you will!
When you get tired of trying, I'll be **still standing still!**"

Then a tall Army Captain, who was standing close by,
Strode right up to Blackie and smiled and said, "Hi!
I can tell you're a horse who admires nature's grandeur.
So come with me now and I say with all candor,
If you'll join my troop in Yosemite Valley,
I'll give you a job there that's right up your alley.

"A job you can do without having to move
So, Blackie, I beg you, please say you'll approve!
And, because you hate change, just to sweeten the deal,
You'll get ten lumps of sugar as part of each meal!"

"Ten lumps of sugar!" thought Blackie. "Great diet!
And I won't have to move? Hey, I might as well try it!"

And try it he did, and the Captain came through,
And gave him a job that he just loved to do…

The Captain explained: "Just stand still as you can,
With me up on your back, near Mount El Capitan,
Or Yosemite Falls, or some tourist's DeSoto,
And let folks who come to the park take our photo!"

Well, the visitors' snapshots showed
sudden improvement;
They were sharp thanks to Blackie's complete
lack of movement,

And, for **efforts** exceeding the mere call of duty,
In helping to showcase Yosemite's beauty,
A trophy was given saluting the **skill**,
Of Blackie, the wonderful horse who **stood still**!

But, when Blackie reached twelve, a doctor came by,
And examined him closely, and said **with a sigh,**
"For this horse's own safety, I'm forced to decide,
That the years have made Blackie too **sway-backed** to ride."

And he sent Blackie off to a place by the Bay,
Where horses **too old** to be ridden could stay.

(And if you've read this far
then you already know,
It took **hundreds of carrots**
to get him to go!)

Well, the Army thought Blackie
would never be sold —
He was simply **too motionless,**
sway-backed, and old —
But in just a few days, they found out
they were wrong,
When a horse-loving **oysterman**
happened along.

"Anthony Connell's my name,"
said the man.
"And I've come here to take a horse
home in my van.
But the horse that I want must
stand **perfectly still.**
By chance, have you got one that
might **fit the bill?**"

"You're in **luck,**" said a soldier,
"it seems that we do.
Come this way, Mr. Connell,
I'll show him to you.
Blackie's his name, but he's
too old to work.
So why would you want him?"
he asked with a **smirk.**

"I don't WANT him to work!" Mr. Connell replied,
In the tone of a man who would not be denied,
"I just want to him to **stand in one spot**
    every day,
While I'm gathering oysters in Richardson Bay,
So that when I glance up to enjoy
    the shore's **scenery,**
I'll know where to find him
    amongst all the **greenery."**
The Army man shrugged and said,
    "Have it your way.
This horse is all yours,
    just as long as you pay."
Mr. Connell said sure, and he wrote out a check,
And grabbed onto the rope tied around
    Blackie's neck.
As he did, he told Blackie,
    "What **pleasure** you'll give,
While I watch you stand still near
    the ark where I live!
My home's up in **Tiburon,** under a ridge...

…With a glorious view of the
Golden Gate Bridge."

Blackie thought, "Standing still? Now how bad could that be…?
No, I don't care for change…but this sounds fine to me!"

So he marched, **without protest,** straight into the van,
And **they drove** 'cross that beautiful Golden Gate span,
(That had only been finished a short time before),
And pulled up at **a field** on the Tiburon shore.

"What a **beautiful place!**" Blackie thought when they got there,

"I simply can't wait just to **stand in one spot** there…

And watch a gull **soar,** or a tree
gently **sway,**
Or the fog **rolling in** from
the hills 'cross the bay,
Or a train on the trestle
up high overhead,
Or a blue heron putting
her nestlings **to bed."**

As the cars on the Tiburon Road passed him by,
All the folks waved at Blackie as if to say "Hi!"
And the people in railroad cars always waved, too,
When the pasture where Blackie stood came into view.

The word quickly spread 'bout the **new horse** in town.
And from all 'round the county young kids headed down,
To the pasture where Blackie could **always be found,**
Standing still, **like a rock**, on the same patch of ground.

They brought **apples**, and **carrots**, and **sugar** to munch on,
For Blackie to breakfast, or sup, or have **lunch** on;

They loved how he'd grab every morsel, and then,
How he'd **chew it up fast** and stop moving again.

And when Blackie slowed down
just to take in the view
The kids saw him do it, and they did it, too,
And they learned, in the process,
what joy can be found
In just standing there quietly looking around.

For year after year, things stayed
almost the same:
The travelers still waved, and
the children still came.
Like Blackie himself, it seemed
time had stood still;
"I love it," thought Blackie, "and I always will!"

But although folks **hardly noticed,**
the town by the bay,
Was actually **changing** a little each day:
More people moved in,
and they brought **cars** and **trucks.**
Leaving **less room** for
flowers, and bunnies, and ducks.

And with everyone driving,
the railroad **closed** down.
And they **tore down** the trestle,
and people in town,
Started griping that **traffic** had
slowed to a crawl.
Thought Blackie: "I don't like these changes at all!"

Then a shopping mall builder exclaimed, "Hey, I know,
A great spot where a new superhighway could go—
And besides, no one lives in this place by the bay,
But a useless old nag who just stands there all day.

"Yes, I'll pave the place over! I'll run a road through it!
I'll put up the world's biggest mall right next to it!
The traffic will flow! I'll be richer by far!"
Said the man, and he laughed and lit up a cigar.

The very next morning, the shopping mall man,
Called the townsfolk together and
        told them his plan.
Their reaction to what he presented was strong;
He thought they would love it, but boy,
        was he wrong!

{fig. 1} BEFORE

TIBURON SHOPPING MALL

TIBURON SHOPPING MALL *(fig. 2)* AFTER

"No way!" said the mayor, wiping sweat
    from his forehead,
"Blackie doesn't like change—and this change is *horrid*!
From Blackie we've learned not to squander
    what's dear to us,
And he, and his pasture, have **nothing to fear** from us!"

Well, the shopping mall mogul left town in a huff,
But the town *had* to deal with that traffic jam stuff,
So they widened the road by the pasture a tad,
And hoped their idea wouldn't make Blackie mad.

Now, it's true that the change in the road
was quite small,
But, of course, Blackie's motto was
"No change at all!"
So he dug in his heels, and they just couldn't goad,
Him to help cut the ribbon to open the road.

They tried carrots, and apples,
and even some fudge,
But nothing they offered could
get him to budge,
So they gave up, and put their food back on the shelf,
And finally the mayor cut the ribbon himself.

The crowd clapped, and said,
"What a great day it's been!"
And they all cheered for Blackie for not giving in.
And as the weeks passed, Blackie savored the sound,
And was prouder than ever that he'd stood his ground.

"I've lived **forty years,**
      and my life's been the best!"
Blackie mused, as he watched **the sun sink**
      in the west,
And he chuckled, recalling the doctor
      who thought him,
Too old at the time Mr. Connell had bought him!

Now for twenty-eight years,
    old Blackie had kept,
Standing up in his pasture each night as he slept.
But this evening felt different,
    and a sudden stiff breeze
Chilled his bones as the winter moon
    rose through the trees.
He said to himself, "Gee, I feel kinda beat."
And he yawned, and lay down in the
    grass 'neath his feet.

Blackie dreamed peaceful dreams
    till the morning, but then,
Found he still felt too weary to stand up again.
They sent for a vet who examined him closely;
When folks asked what was wrong,
    the vet answered morosely,
"He's plain tuckered out,"
    and he started to weep,
And the very next night Blackie died in his sleep.

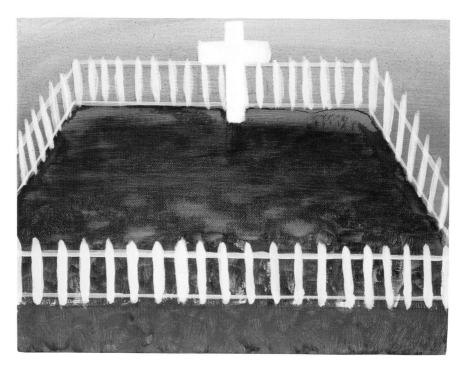

Well, Blackie was buried, right there where he lay,
In his beautiful pasture by Richardson Bay,

And Tiburon's families filed by him for hours,
Bringing apples, and carrots, and sugar, and flowers,
Which they carefully placed, as they fought back their tears,
On the grave of the horse they had loved all those years.

Then the newspaper published a big editorial
Suggesting the town build a Blackie **memorial.**
"A statue," they said, "of our old, sway-backed steed
Standing proud in his pasture is just what we need,
The statue won't move—just like Blackie before it;
It'll be our **town symbol,** and folks will adore it."

Well, the statue was built, and if you **stop** and stare

Out at Blackie's old pasture, you'll feel he's still there...

He fought against change; now his field never will....

Thanks to Blackie, the wonderful horse who stood still.

EPILOGUE

Blackie was born in Kansas and came west to California, where he appeared in the Salinas Rodeo and served as a U.S. Cavalry mounted patrol horse at Yosemite National Park. When he was 12 years old, he retired to his private pasture in Tiburon, California where he stood (rarely moving) for the next 28 years. Visitors of all ages regularly fed him carrots, sugar, and apples, and most everyone passing by would smile or wave to him.

Blackie died on February 27, 1966; a simple, white cross marks his grave. The Tiburon Peninsula Foundation (TPF), a volunteer group originally founded to preserve Blackie's pasture and dedicated to creating a sense of community in the area, used a gift from the family of Tiburon's first mayor, Gordon Strawbridge, to erect a life-sized bronze sculpture of Blackie on the very spot where he stood for so many years. With his statue, made by sculptor Albert Guibara, Blackie still has the power to make his visitors smile.

To paraphrase Robert Browning's poem, "Blackie's in his pasture—all's right with the world."